Published by Spirit Marketing, LLC
706 Broadway, Suite 101, Kansas City, MO 64105
hellospiritmarketing.com

ISBN 978-1-944953-38-6

This special edition was printed for Kohl's, Inc. (for distribution on behalf of Kohl's Cares, LLC, its wholly owned subsidiary) by Spirit Marketing, LLC.

Printed in Heshan, China

Kohl's, Inc.
Style: JHD1-6269
Factory: 208840
08/22-11/22

Bunny woke up one beautiful morning and saw that the field was covered with flowers. **"Hello FLOWERS! Hello SPRING!"**

Bunny wanted to pick Mom a special bouquet of her favorite blossoms.

Over the hill, Bunny saw some friendly ears waving above the green grass.
"Hello MOM!"

But it wasn't Bunny's mom—those big tall ears belonged to Mama Kangaroo, and her joey too!

"OH—Hello 'ROOS!" Bunny said as they bounced.

"Hello BUNNY!" they exclaimed. "Your mom probably went into the garden!"

In the garden, Bunny spotted a familiar pink
whiskery nose in a huge flowering bush.
"Hello MOM!"

But again, it wasn't Bunny's mom!
Those whiskers belonged to Daddy
Cat and his two cuddly kittens.

"OH—**Hello KiTTies!**" Bunny said as they played.

"**Hello BUNNY!**" they meowed. "Your mom probably went into the forest!"

Bunny saw more blooms near the edge of the trees—and a fluffy white tail sticking out of the leaves. **"Hello MOM!"**

But the fluffy tail belonged to Granny Deer, grazing with the littlest fawn.

"OH—Hello DeeR!"
Bunny said as they munched.

"Hello BUNNY!"
they replied. "Your mom probably went back to your nest!"

On the way back to the nest, Bunny saw in the distance two big tall ears, a pink whiskery nose, and a fluffy white tail...

"Hello MOM!"
Bunny said with a hop.
"I've looked for you
high and low."